Where Did My Love Go?

Jesse Cruz
Haleigh Cruz
Mariah Cruz

Published by Pen It Publications in the U.S.A.

713-526-3989

www.penitpublications.com

ISBN: 978-1-63984-351-0

Illustrations by Sanghamitra Dasgupta

I keep asking myself,
Where did my love go?

There are many people
I love who have left.

Mommy told me that an accident happened.

But her sad face makes it seem like it was something worse than getting gum stuck in my hair, or scraping my knee on the pavement.

She looks like she wants to be left alone. Every day.

What really happened?
Nobody's telling me, I'm so confused.

Why did this happen? I thought only old people died.

I remember being told that everyone on earth will someday leave.

I wonder where that place is?

Sometimes I hug my stuffed animals and pretend it's my dad.

My dad died. When will
I see him again?

My mom is dead
and I really miss
her.

R.I.P

I still think my teacher who died last year will come back to life.

Last year my
sister died
and I am
angry.

I drew some pictures to remember my grandma.

There is no way that my cousin is dead, I just saw him last week.

Some days I am happy.

but then I remember
that my friend died.

I sure do miss my uncle.

I hear songs and I think about my uncle.

I enjoyed the good times
with my aunt.

I see some pretty flowers
and think about my aunt.

I really miss my cat and my fish.

Sometimes I believe it's my fault that my dog died.

I bet you if I am a good kid my best friend will come back to life.

Maybe I should have done something different and they would still be alive.

I still set the dinner table
with the empty chair
just in case my grandpa
comes back to visit.

I am reminded that he's not coming back and now I am confused.

He still hasn't come back. My sadness has been going on for months.

I have a hard time
sleeping or eating.

I get really scared when mommy or daddy go to work.

I hope they
don't die.

Today at recess I was having so much fun and then I started crying for no reason.

I think I still miss them.

When will I stop being sad? I hope it's soon.

People say "I am here for you
if you ever want to talk about it."

But instead of talking, I cry or stay
quiet.

I also hear "I am sorry for your loss.
I am here to help."

My mom told me
that many people
in our family are
going to be sad for
a while.

It's okay to feel sad
when something bad
happens.

Don't apologize for how
you feel, just make sure
to tell someone.

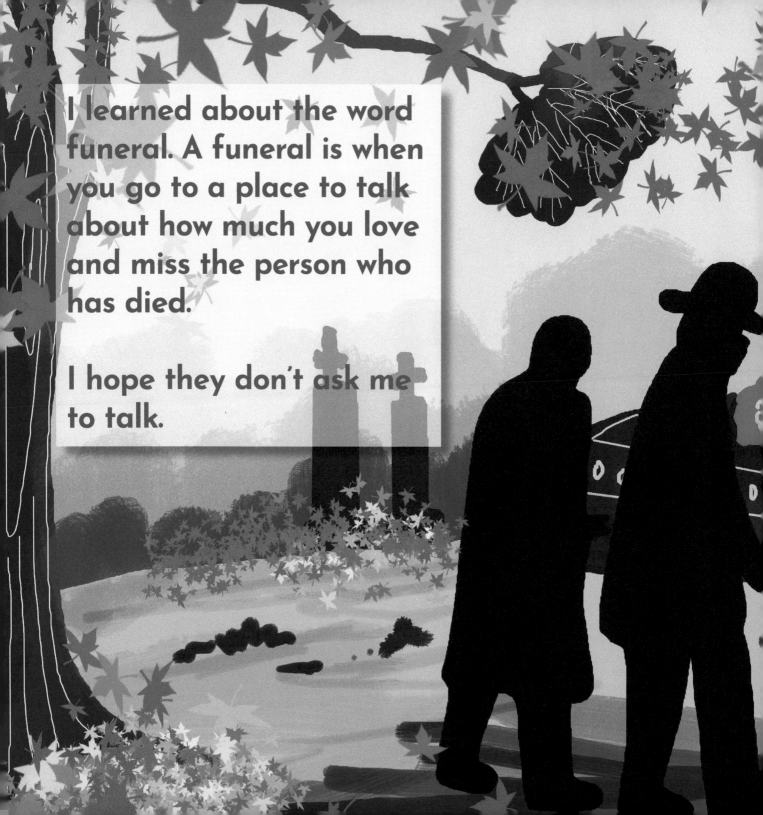

I learned about the word funeral. A funeral is when you go to a place to talk about how much you love and miss the person who has died.

I hope they don't ask me to talk.

I want to remember my family who is no longer here. My dad showed me several pictures of the people who have died.

I had some great memories with them. For some of them I don't have any memories at all.

As a family we planted a tree to remember my sister.

My mom and dad have been crying a lot. I don't want them to be sad anymore.

I hope they stop crying soon. I am going to be a good kid so they never cry again.

My brother said it's going to take some time until we all aren't sad anymore.

But I am not sad anymore and the rest of my family is. But they said that it's okay.

We keep having many visitors at the house. Every day more and more people come over.

We are trying to go back to normal, but something doesn't feel right.

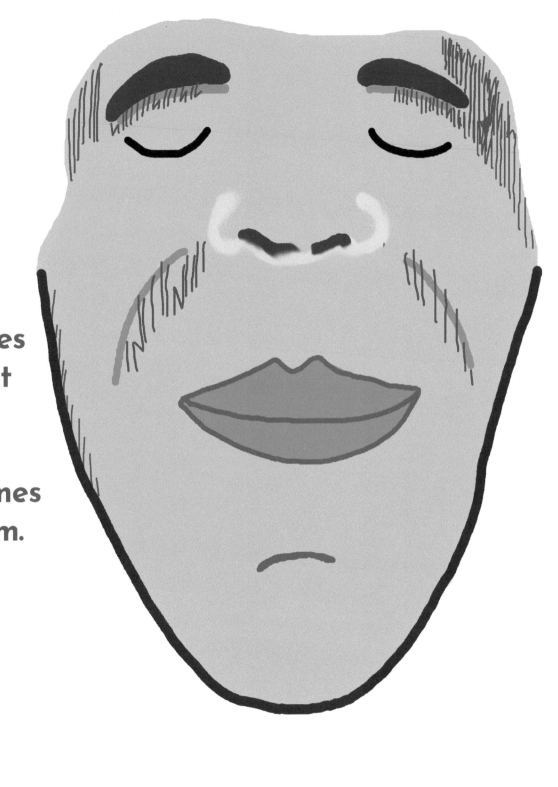

Sometimes
we just sit
quietly.

Other times
we scream.

I have been having a lot of fun lately.
I am smiling and laughing again.
We now have less visitors than before.

I am now back in school and my parents are back to work.

I was given this awesome fishing pole to remember my dad.

Every time I go fishing I remember him.

Some people tell me they know how I am feeling.

I don't believe them because I don't even know how I am feeling.

My parents signed me up for a class called counseling.

It's a safe place to talk about my feelings.

The counselor is kind. I am glad I can talk to them.

I have so many questions and finally got an answer to my question Where did my love go?

The people I love are in my heart and my heart is always with me.

When people die they go to a place called heaven.

I have heard it's perfect there. They say it's full of love and everyone is happy.

I hope to go there someday and see everyone I love.

I am now happy because one day I get to see them in heaven.

ABOUT THE AUTHOR

Jesse Cruz is a Professional Speaker, Storytelling and Personal Development Coach, Best-Selling Author, Veteran and Youth Advocate. He is the founder and CEO Merge Worldwide. Jesse inspires others to overcome their challenges and achieve their goals. Jesse speaks and coaches at events all over the world! His passion is to empower people to share their story to heal from loss and grow into their goals. Jesse motivates people to achieve their true potential through his coaching programs. Jesse empowers his clients to overcome adversity and develop success in their personal and professional lives. He is the Author of "Live Your Dash" a book written to guide people to freedom by discovering their purpose. His latest book Losing Faith, Finding Hope is a guide to inspire hope and overcome loss through healing. Jesse's passion and ability to connect with his audience is unmatched and have made him a highly sought-out speaker for top organizations including the Ronald Mcdonald House. He was honored with the "#1 Dad award from his daughters. He and his wife Desire, believe in spreading H.O.P.E. by Helping Other People Everyday. Jesse is a man of faith and a pleasure to work with. If you are an event planner looking for an inspiring, highly motivated and passionate speaker for your next event, then Jesse Cruz is the speaker for you.

CPSIA information can be obtained
at www.ICGtesting.com
Printed in the USA
BVHW022012251022
650285BV00002B/3